¡FIESTA!

By **Ginger Foglesong Guy**

Pictures by **René King Moreno**

Greenwillow Books New York

Pastels, watercolors, and colored pencils
were used to create the full-color artwork.
The text type is Kabel Ultra Bold.

Library of Congress Cataloging-in-Publication Data

Guy, Ginger Foglesong.
¡Fiesta! / by Ginger Foglesong Guy;
pictures by René King Moreno.
    p.   cm.
"Greenwillow Books"
English and Spanish.
Summary: Bilingual text describes a children's party
and provides practice counting in English and Spanish.
[1. Parties—Fiction. 2. Counting. 3. Spanish language materials—Bilingual.]
I. Moreno, René King, ill. II. Title.
PZ73.G84 1996 [E]—dc20 95-35848 CIP AC

ISBN-13: 978-0-688-14331-2 (trade bdg.) ISBN-10: 0-688-14331-8 (trade bdg.)
ISBN-13: 978-0-06-088226-6 (pbk.) ISBN-10: 0-06-088226-3 (pbk.)

First Edition   18 19 20 SCP 22 21 20 19

 Greenwillow Books
An Imprint of HarperCollins*Publishers*

rayo

Rayo is an imprint of HarperCollins Publishers Inc.

For my mother and father, who gave me Mexico,
and my brother and sisters, who shared it with me
—G. F. G.

For Zakkary, Spencer, and Anna
—R. K. M.

Una canasta
One basket

Dos trompetas
Two horns

¿Qué más?

What else?

Tres animalitos
Three little animals

¿Qué más?
What else?

Cuatro aviones
Four airplanes

¿Qué más?
What else?

Cinco trompos
Five tops

¿Qué más?
What else?

Seis chicles
Six pieces of gum

¿Qué más?   What else?

Siete silbatos

Seven whistles

¿Qué más?
What else?

Ocho anillos

Eight rings

¿Qué más?
What else?

Nueve dulces
Nine candies

¿Qué más?
What else?

Diez serpentinas

Ten streamers

¡Niños!
Children!

One! ¡Uno!

Two! ¡Dos!

Three! ¡Tres!

Four! ¡Cuatro!

Five! ¡CINCO!

Six! ¡Seis!

Seven! ¡Siete!

Eight! ¡Ocho!

Nine! ¡Nueve!

Ten! ¡Diez!